P9-DHS-440

JUBAL'S WISH

STORY BY

AUDREY WOOD

PICTURES BY

DON WOOD

THE BLUE SKY PRESS

An Imprint of Scholastic Inc. • New York

THE BLUE SKY PRESS

Library of Congress catalog card number: 99-086372
ISBN 0-439-16964-X
10 9 8 7 6 5 4 3 2 1   0/0 01 02 03 04
www.audreywood.com
Printed in Singapore   46
First printing, October 2000
Designed by Don Wood and Kathleen Westray

TO BONNIE AND ZACH

Once upon a bright and sunny day,
Jubal Bullfrog skipped down
the flower path. He was so happy
his feet barely touched the ground.

Before long, he came to the cottage of Gerdy Toad and her seven toadlets. *Whackity-whack!* Gerdy was outside beating a dirty old rug with her broom.

"A happy sunny day to you, dear friend!" Jubal exclaimed.

"What's so happy about it?" Gerdy snapped. "The toadlets are into everything, and my house is a mess. For all I care, it could be raining!"

"But I've made a picnic to share," Jubal said, holding up his basket.

"Picnic! I don't have time for that," Gerdy grumped. "Work, work, work, that's all I ever do."

Gerdy Toad heaved the rug over her shoulder and stomped into her cottage.

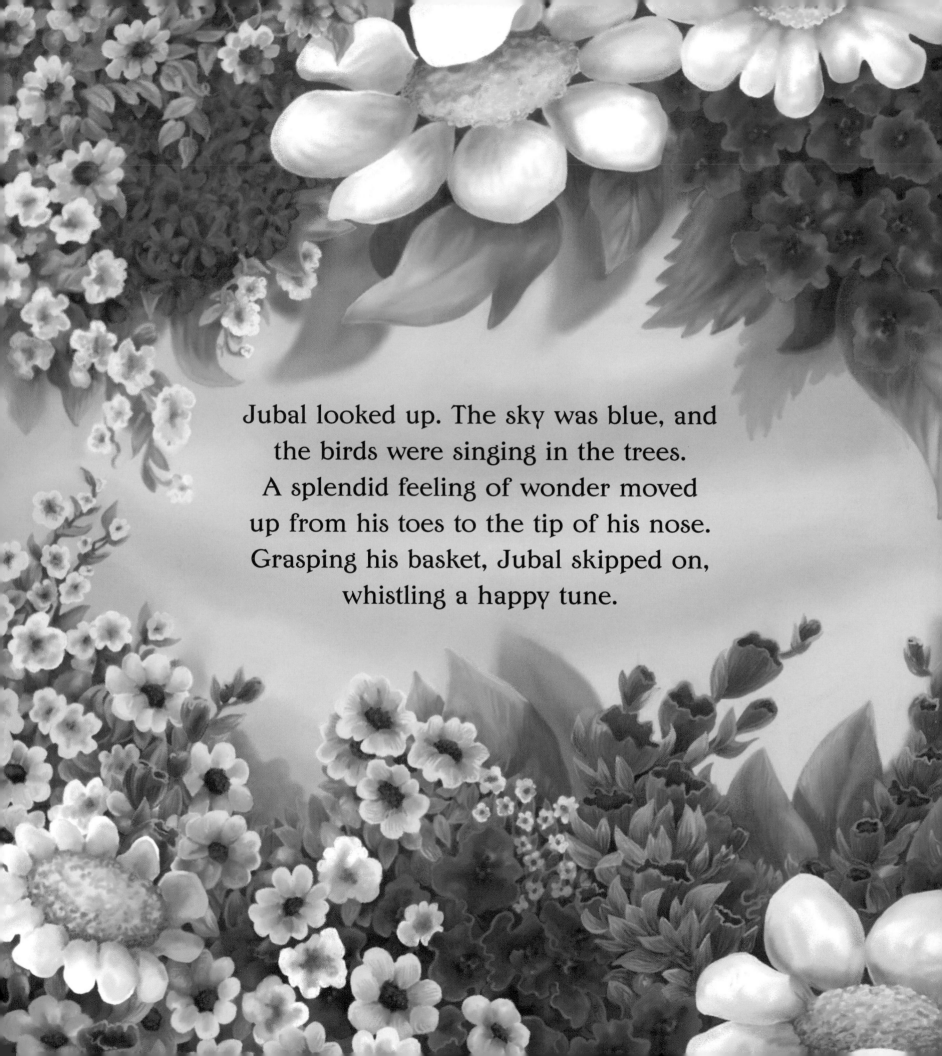

Jubal looked up. The sky was blue, and
the birds were singing in the trees.
A splendid feeling of wonder moved
up from his toes to the tip of his nose.
Grasping his basket, Jubal skipped on,
whistling a happy tune.

Down by the river, Jubal found Captain Dalbert Lizard lounging in the shade of his sailboat, the *Molly Bee*.

"A happy sunny day to you, dear friend!" Jubal called.

The lizard opened one eye and sighed. "My happy days are over," he said. "Once I was a great captain, bound for adventure with a fine crew. But now no one wants to sail in an old boat with an old captain."

"I know just what you need," Jubal said, holding up his basket. "A picnic always makes everything better."

"Sorry, Jubal," Captain Dalbert said as he slowly climbed the ladder to his cabin. "I'm not in the mood."

For a moment, Jubal thought, "Maybe I should be unhappy, too." But the fresh grass and sweet flowers smelled so good. Jubal plopped down beneath a daisy and took a deep breath. He leaned back, closed his eyes, and said, "I wish there was something I could do to make my friends as happy as I am on this glorious day."

A butterfly came dancing over his 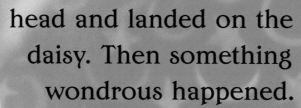 head and landed on the daisy. Then something wondrous happened.

A great hand reached down
and scooped Jubal
high up into the air.
"Do you need a wish?"
a wizard asked
the startled bullfrog.

Reaching into his pocket, the wizard brought out a small, twinkling star. "It's a wish," he said, "and it's yours if you want it."

"A wish!" Jubal exclaimed. "Do they really come true?"

"Dreams and wishes, wishes and dreams," the wizard said with a wink. "Sometimes they work, and sometimes they don't. You never know how they'll turn out in the end."

The bullfrog took the twinkling star and held it next to his heart. "I wish Gerdy Toad's housework was done, and her toadlets were well-behaved, and Captain Dalbert had his adventures back. That's my wish."

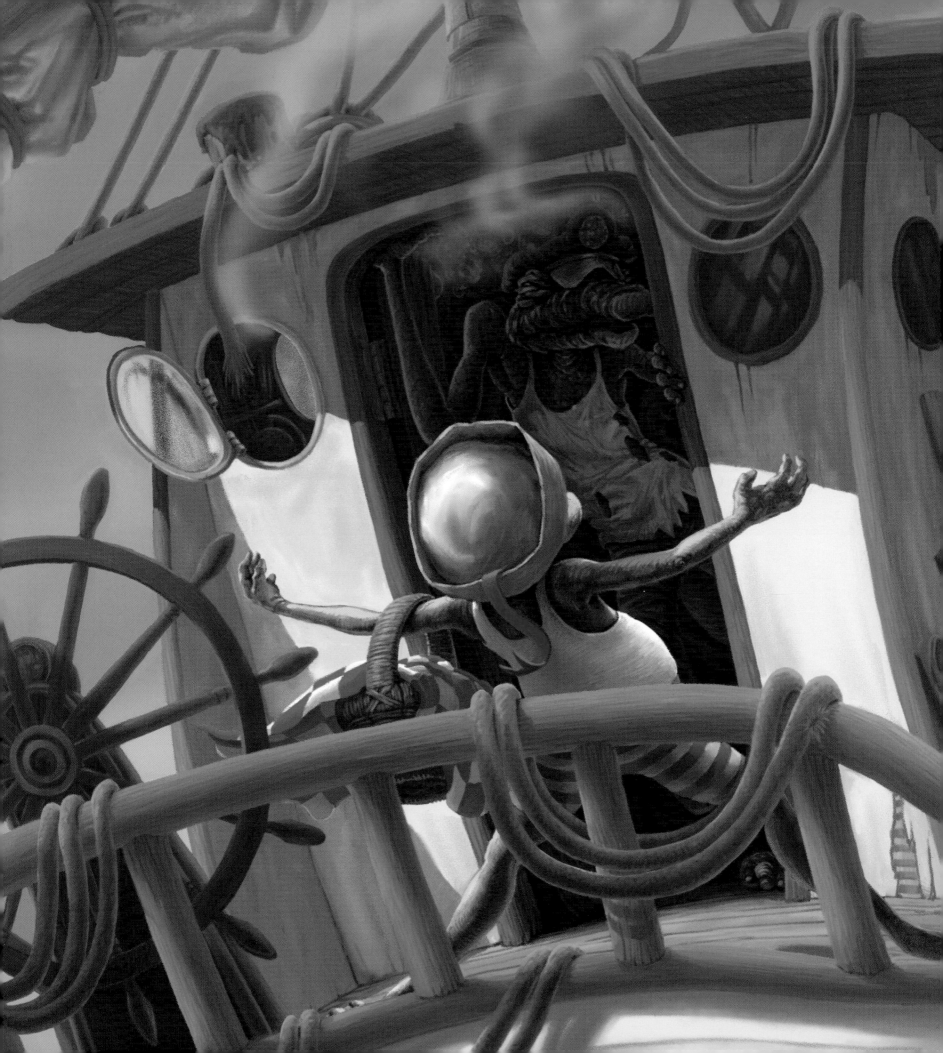

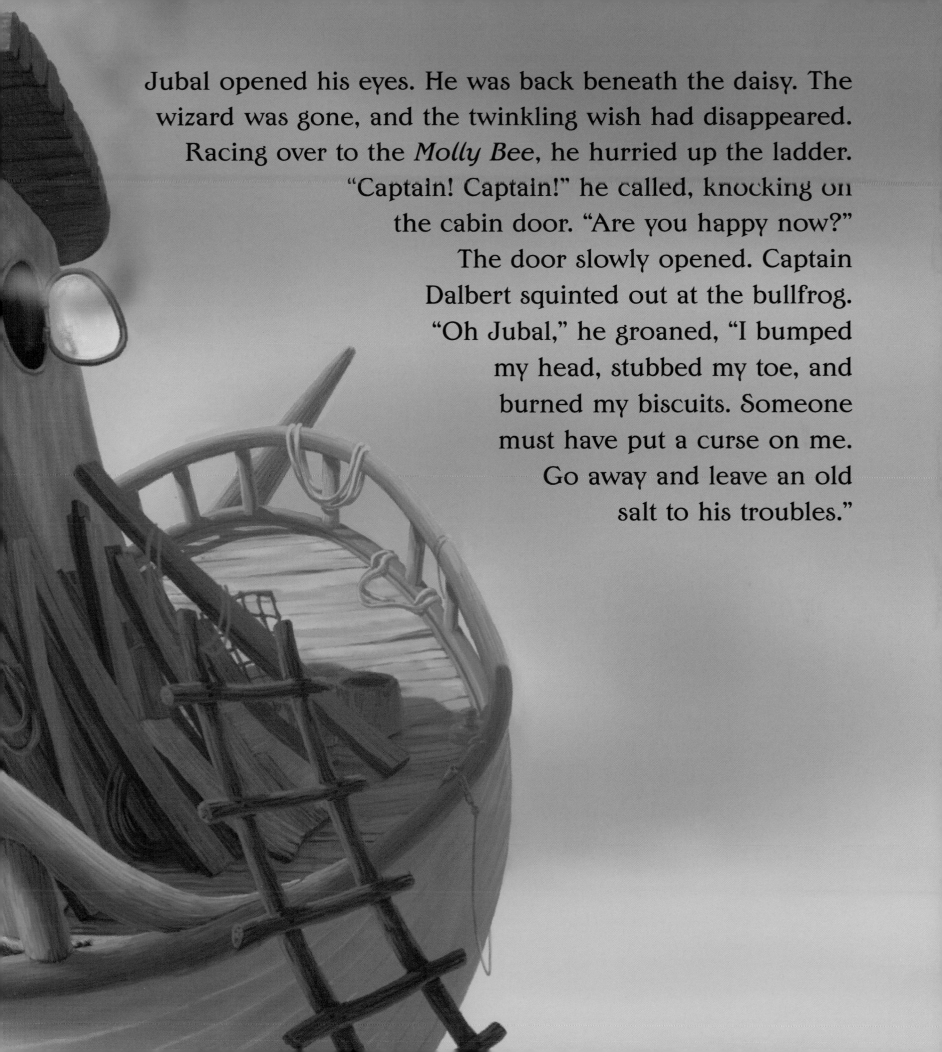

Jubal opened his eyes. He was back beneath the daisy. The wizard was gone, and the twinkling wish had disappeared. Racing over to the *Molly Bee*, he hurried up the ladder. "Captain! Captain!" he called, knocking on the cabin door. "Are you happy now?" The door slowly opened. Captain Dalbert squinted out at the bullfrog. "Oh Jubal," he groaned, "I bumped my head, stubbed my toe, and burned my biscuits. Someone must have put a curse on me. Go away and leave an old salt to his troubles."

As Jubal walked back up the path,
a dark cloud gathered in the sky, hiding the sun.
When the bullfrog passed Gerdy Toad's cottage
he heard her yelling inside, "Stop squabbling!
What a mess! Pick up your toys!"
Thunder boomed, and lightning flashed.

Before long, Jubal came to a large toadstool. He climbed up and sat down to think. "My wish didn't work. That wizard tricked me. Captain Dalbert and Gerdy are more miserable than ever. And what has happened to my happy sunny day?"

A tear trickled down his cheek just as the first drop of rain plopped onto his nose.

Jubal sobbed, and the rain poured down.

The rain made deep puddles, the puddles ran together and formed a stream, and the stream grew wider and soon became a rushing river. Jubal didn't notice what was happening until icy water washed over his toes.

"Oh, dear!" he cried. "It's a flood! I'll be swept away!"

Great waves rolled toward the bullfrog.
"Help! Somebody save me!" he shouted.
"I'm stranded!"

A faint voice called in the distance, "Jubal . . . where are you?"

"I'm over here!" he yelled, trying to see through the blinding rain.

A struggling sailboat bobbed into view.

"Hang on, Jubal!" an anxious voice called. "We're almost there!"

The sailboat fought its way
through the storm until
it struck the toadstool
with a bump. Gerdy
and her toadlets
pulled Jubal from
the stormy water
just in time.

"Welcome aboard, Matey!" Captain Dalbert shouted as he slapped his friend on the back. "What a day, eh? I haven't seen this much action since the typhoon of forty-nine. Good work, toadlets! You are a fine crew!"

"Aye aye, Captain," the toadlets agreed.

"Oh Jubal! I'm so glad you're safe!" Gerdy Toad said, hugging him. "It's a miracle! Our cottage floated away, and Captain Dalbert rescued us all."

"Gracious!" Jubal exclaimed. "What will you do now?"

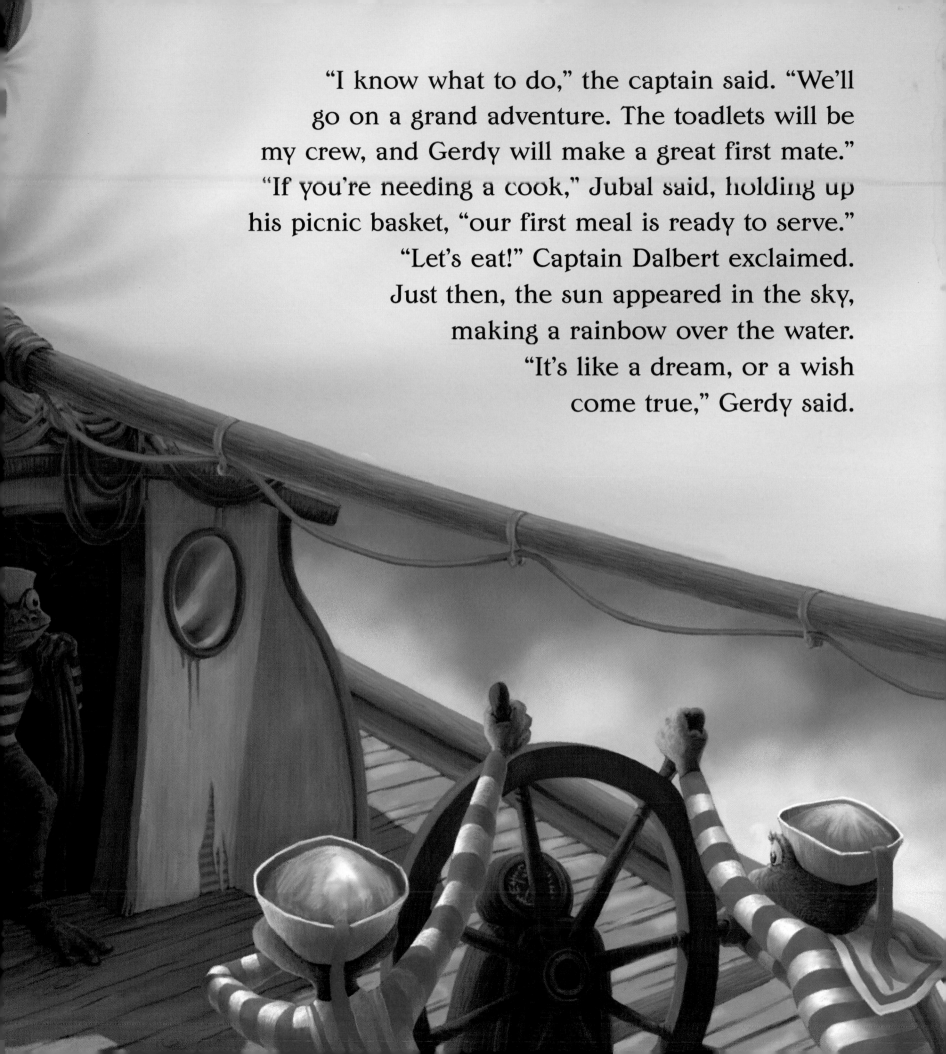

"I know what to do," the captain said. "We'll go on a grand adventure. The toadlets will be my crew, and Gerdy will make a great first mate."

"If you're needing a cook," Jubal said, holding up his picnic basket, "our first meal is ready to serve."

"Let's eat!" Captain Dalbert exclaimed. Just then, the sun appeared in the sky, making a rainbow over the water.

"It's like a dream, or a wish come true," Gerdy said.

"Dreams and wishes, wishes and dreams,"
Jubal said with a wink. "Sometimes they work,
and sometimes they don't. You never know
how they'll turn out in the end."